WENDY WI[...]
AND THE IMPOSSIBLE
GHOSTS

By
Kelly Hambly

Chapter One

Pluto looks gorgeous tonight. Not *that* Pluto, the one demoted from a planet, Pluto. I'm talking about my fluffy ginger cat sitting on the garden wall basking in the moonlight - my best friend, Pluto. In fact, she's my only friend in the entire cosmos, and I love her so much.

As I adjust the lens of my binoculars, I zoom in on her and the cool, white glow surrounding her because at first glance she looks like a cat ghost! I chuckle at this because I don't believe in ghosts or anything paranormal, unlike my mother who makes a living from writing spooky stories. We couldn't be so different, my mother and I, but she is my favourite person in the whole world even though I think some of her ideas are just plain ridiculous.

I then pan my binoculars skywards, hoping to catch the meteor shower expected this evening, but so far there has been nothing. Not one shooting star so far. I lower the binoculars, slightly disappointed and catch a glimpse of Pluto also looking displeased although I don't think it's about the meteors more like wanting her supper and warmth. The way I feel, I could just sit in front of the fire with a mug of cocoa and watch Sky at Night, but we're going away soon for a holiday. It's nowhere exotic. It's just a small village about fifteen miles from here.

'Well, this seems like a waste of time, doesn't it? Shall we go inside?'

She lifts her sleepy head and miaows as if to say yes, *feed me and warm me, you silly child!* However, I'm determined to catch one so I can make a wish. I can't tell you my wish or it won't come true - and I need it to come true because it would mean the world to me.

'Wendy, it's time to leave,' calls mum from the patio doors. I turn to see my mum heading to the car on the drive, so I scoop Pluto into my arms and trudge across the grass. We're staying with my aunt Wilhelmina while mum is on her week-long book tour up and down the country.

'Have you got my rucksack?' I ask as I bundle Pluto into the car, and as I do so I get a sense to look upwards at the sky and just over the tip of the skeletal tree, I see a quick flash of a meteor, hurriedly close my eyes, and make my wish. Now I'm ready for my holiday to the Black Mountains and Auntie's peculiar Manor House. I say peculiar because it's old, with black brickwork and has an eerie feel as if you're being watched, but of course there's nobody watching you – that's just stupid. The only people who rent it these days are paranormal investigators and some have been known to leave in the middle of the night terrified. That's how auntie makes her living, also from the paranormal. I sometimes think I'm the only sane person among them. Fortunately, I have never experienced such things. Even if I did, there surely must be a logical explanation. Surely.

Driving down the windy, narrow country lanes, I peer out of the open window and look up at the sky. It's so dark in the countryside that I can see many constellations I wouldn't normally be able to at home due to the light pollution. I rummage in the glovebox for a pen and make a quick note in my book of what I've observed. When I'm older, I plan to study space science and become a world-renowned expert who has their own television show. I know, I can dream, right? But dreams have been known to come true.

'We're almost there, Wend,' Mum says. 'Are you sure you don't want to come with me? You can change your mind, you know.'

'No thanks, Mum. I have plans,' I patted my rucksack on my lap that contains my brand-new telescope and my books.

'You do know Wilhelmina's house is...'

'Haunted? Yeah, I know, Mum, and I told you, I'm a scientist. I don't believe in that rubbish.'

Mum laughs. 'Well, that's your opinion and you're entitled to your opinion, but if anything happens, anything at all, you *will* call me?'

Mum often uses her sister's house as inspiration for her work. Well, I say it's her sisters, but Witchspell manor belongs to our family. Mum chose to live in a modern house, and I can't say that I blame her. Her latest novel is a tale about a ghost who terrifies the living to the point they moved halfway across the world. Only to find that the ghost travelled with them attaching itself to an antique vase and caused all sorts of mayhem. Mum sold hundreds of copies in a day, and it shot to number one on the Amazon charts. Since then, she has been asked to do talks and signings all over the country.

As we come up the drive, the heavy wooden door opens, and Aunt Wilhelmina's stick insect frame steps out of the house. She's a tall woman in her mid-forties with long black hair and a silver streak that runs down it on one side. Mum says she's never left the Goth phase she took up in the early 1990s. Personally, I think she'd make a great Morticia Addams. She waves as we park the car beside the water fountain and walks up to the door beaming like a Cheshire cat at me.

'Ah there she is, my favourite niece and her cat,' she pulls me in for a hug as if she hadn't seen me for years. It was only last week she met us at mum's book signing in the local bookshop in town. She seems to be acting a little weird tonight, and I have no idea why. Or maybe she's just glad of the company. It can't be much fun sharing a huge house with spiders and dare I say it, ghosts – if there is such a thing, which there isn't.

'It's okay if she stays here, isn't it?'' asks mum, getting my case from the boot. 'I know it's Halloween soon and... well, you've things to do...'

'Of course it's alright, we'll have a fab time, don't worry.' She takes my case off mum, and I haul my rucksack over my shoulder. 'I've got plans for Halloween, I'm sure she'll enjoy, Paige. The only thing I'm worried about is...'

Mum glares at her and thinks I don't notice. 'I don't think it's necessary to go into details, is it? I mean, she's been perfectly fine here before plus she doesn't believe in any of that, so I haven't bothered her with the story,' she whispers but it's pointless because I have fantastic hearing and heard every word.

I'm standing listening to this weird conversation mum and auntie are having and I'm not really liking it. What's their secret? And what are they not telling me? Maybe this will be my mission here: to find out.

Anyway, Halloween... I haven't celebrated Halloween since I was nine-years-old when I declared to mum that I had enough of this childish nonsense, I'm an astrophysicist in training now, but she still bought me a witch's hat and a trick or treat bag she'd fill because I never left the house knocking strangers' doors. If I'm honest, I did enjoy the sweets. That's the only thing I love about Halloween these days.

'I will only be a week, so have a nice time, alright?' Mum hugs me and kisses Pluto goodbye then heads back down the drive. 'Have a nice time you two, see you soon,' mum waves. 'Oh, and Wilhelmina,' she yells from the wound down window, 'let me know if anything happens.'

'Will do, now off you go. Don't worry about a thing I have everything under control.'

What does she have under control? She can't control the big old house she lives in I think to myself looking at the over spilling bins by the door.

'Come on, Wend, let's have some cocoa and a catch-up chat.'

'I'm just letting Pluto out to the toilet, I'll be in soon,' I say but Auntie's face paled – even paler than it already was.

'No, best if you come in, Wend. Pluto will be fine.' She ushers me through the door, turns to lock it and gestures me down the hall to the kitchen. As I walk the long, dark hallway, paintings of old family members watch me as I pass. I wouldn't mind them nosing so much, but they're rather scary looking or maybe they're painted to look that way. I never bothered to ask. I don't know much about the Witchspell family. Mum never talks about them. It's always been me, my mother and aunt after their parents had passed away. My dad on the other hand left when I was born so he has never been around either.

Entering Auntie's kitchen, it never ceases to amaze me how huge it is, with shelves of varying-coloured bottles, containing who knew what, pots and pans dangling from the ceiling and the enormous AGA cooker, which was always on, wafting delicious smells of fresh bread and cakes. Usually there'd be something bubbling in a pan on the stove too. They've been there for as long as I can remember and I'm only fourteen.

'Here you go, my homemade hot chocolate,' she gets the ladle out of a small cauldron on the AGA, scoops in a mugful and hands it to me. I've been looking forward to this all week because she makes it from real chocolate not that stuff you buy in tubs. 'I thought we could have a chat, Wend, is that alright?' She sits next to me at the table and stirs her chocolate in her pumpkin shaped mug.

'Is everything alright, Auntie?' I ask, feeling a little on edge. She certainly seems spooked tonight.

'Wend, what do you know about our family? Has your mother told you anything at all? Anything about our Halloween? Knowing her she hasn't.'

'No. She never talks about our family's history. Why is this important now?' I ask, thinking how quickly she brought this up considering I've been here less than five minutes and mum had asked her to keep quiet about something.

She lowers her mug so slowly as if she were building up to a dramatic conclusion. I don't know what it is about auntie today, but she ought to take up acting. Hollywood would love her.

'Your mother made me promise not to mention anything, but unfortunately I'm left with no choice...'

Just as Auntie was about to tell me something I see in my peripheral vision, a bottle about to slide off the shelf.

'Oh quick,' I reach out my hand just as it topples off the shelf and lands in my palm, wobbling a bit and then I grab it with the other. 'No damage, see?' I say to my aunt who is now standing with her hands covering her mouth. I don't know what the big deal is, she has plenty of other bottles and they all appear to be empty.

'Well done, Wend, well done. Please put it back carefully and I'll show you to your room,' she says, jittery. 'Oh, by the way, part of the house has been rented this evening by a paranormal group, so please try to stay out of their way.'

'So, what were you going to tell me?' I ask, desperate to know.

As we're about to walk up the wooden staircase, she pauses and takes a deep breath. 'You know what? It's nothing. It's just me and your mum being ridiculous that's all. The house is old and has lots of history, some not so pleasant I'm sorry to say.'

'Oh?

'Yeah, but it doesn't really concern you,' she says and mutters under her breath that she hoped not. I don't think I was meant to hear that.

Chapter Two

This part of the house is dimly lit, it's almost like living during the Second World War when they had blackouts. And if I'm not mistaken this house was used by the military for training in 1940. I know this because I looked up the place on the internet. There's also one other weird story attached to the place, but I'm sure it's just nonsense – urban legends as they call them involving witches. Auntie says it costs too much to run a house this size and since she lives on her own, there's no point putting on all the lights or heating, so the house is as cold as the Arctic and is dark as the night sky. Except tonight she says she has made an exception and put the radiators on in my room because "it's Baltic" in there, apparently.

'I've made up the room in the attic, is that alright?' She grabs my suitcase and I nod my approval. 'It's out of the way of the investigators as I'm sure you don't want to be involved in that, do you?'

'Not really. But the attic is perfect for my stargazing.' I scoop Pluto under my arm and ascend the wooden staircase, not one, but three that wind around until I get to the top floor. Out of the arch window on the landing I see the moon and its light spilling onto the back garden. The hedges are shaped into a maze with a fountain at the centre and beyond that there is mountains and trees as far as they eye can see.

'You should be comfortable up here. This room used to belong to your mother and I,' she says, carrying the case up the step ladder to the attic.

'Did it really?' It dawns on me at this point that I really don't know much about my family, especially my mother's side and I wonder why this is. Pluto jumps out of my arms, hissing at something down the corridor.

'Oh Pluto, don't be daft, it's probably just a mouse.'

'There are no mice here, thank you very much,' says Auntie, a little affronted. 'I scrub this place clean every day.'

I doubt that very much considering the size of the place. It'd probably take you six weeks just to clean all the bedrooms.

I walk up the steps and enter the room. Auntie goes into her cardigan pocket and pulls out a bulb. 'I'll put this in the lamp for you. It should be enough light but if it isn't I can bring you another lamp.'

'Thank you,' I say, relieved I wasn't going to spend my time here in the dark. Not that I'm afraid of the dark, it's just that I have some new books I want to read on blackholes and the solar system.

'So, there we are,' she says, looking pleased with her handiwork. 'If you need anything you know you can go and get it. The kitchen is stocked and there is plenty of fizzy pop and junk food, but don't tell your mother I gave it to you,' she winks.

'Thanks.' I flounce on the bed. Pluto comes to join me and curls up next to my leg which is unusual as she normally loves to sleep on the windowsill. I get my book from my bag and sit up against the headboard, inspecting the room. The radiator under the window clangs and splutters, but no heat emerges from it. I think everything in this house has given up, even the curtains hang limp and dusty. Opening my book on blackholes which I had signed by the author, an incredibly famous astrophysicist from the telly, I feel an icy chill creep along my hands, so I get under the covers for warmth with my torch. Out of nowhere I hear feet across the landing. "Is that you, Auntie?" But there was no reply. A few moments later, the door opens. 'Here you go, Wend.' She puts a glass down on the dresser and I inwardly sigh with relief.

'Was that you on the landing a few moments ago?' I ask.

Her sharply pencilled-in eyebrows knit together. 'No. Why?'

'Thought I heard footsteps, that's all. Probably the pipes,' I say.

'Possibly,' she replies, unconvincingly and fusses with my blankets. 'If you're cold in the night, there are more blankets in the cupboard down the hall.'

'Thanks.'

'No bother. See you in the morning. Night.' She closes the door behind her and then my mobile rings. It's mum.

'Anything exciting happen?'

'Apart from feet on the landing or the pipes creaking, no.'

'Oh footsteps. Sounds like it's getting exciting there. Let me know what happens, Wend, okay, and maybe we'll have a chat.'

A chat? A chat about what? I laugh at mum's words and say I would go and (jokingly) investigate, whilst I went to get another blanket. Suddenly, the temperature seems to drop again and only in certain places. This isn't normal, is it? Then again it is October.

'Come on, Pluto.'

Pluto looks up as if to say you must be joking and snuggles back down into the blanket.

I open the door and climb down the steps into a dark hallway fumbling for a light switch, but there isn't one I could find so I switch the torch on the mobile instead.

I'm barely inches from the ladder when I feel, what appears to be a string of cotton on my face. Thinking it was a spiderweb, I run my hand over my face to remove it but there isn't anything there. *Weird*. I creep down the hall, passing another bedroom and then find the cupboard. As I open the door, I see a shadow pass in my peripheral vision and look back. 'Hello?' Must be one of the paranormal investigators Auntie was talking about.

'Uhm.'

'Hello? Sorry if I'm disturbing your investigation. I'm just getting extra blankets,' I say. 'I'm not a spectre, honest,' I snigger.

There's no reply. I shine the torch in the direction of the voice, and sure enough there was nobody there. If mum were here, she'd have said it was a ghost, but rational old me knows it's the creaky old house. I tuck the blanket under my arms and curiously walks to the turning in the hall that led to the older part of the house. Walking along, minding my own business, I hear beeping and see flashes of red and blue lights on the floor.

'We've got a shadow,' someone shrieks, and as I walk towards the voices, they let out a blood curdling scream scaring me to the point I jump back in fright. 'It's okay, my aunt owns the house,' I say, but the two people standing stock still in front of me say nothing. 'I'm not a ghost.' I reassure them. 'I'm flesh and blood, like you.'

'You are?' says the young boy who didn't look much older than me.

'How many ghosts have you caught with mobile phones?' I wave mine around to make a point. 'I mean if they did you could easily call up the afterlife for a chat, couldn't you?' I laugh.

'Sorry about that,' he says. 'I'm William and this is my dad.'

'Nice to meet you both. I'm Wendy, Wilhelmina's niece.'

'And nice to meet you. I'm sorry if we gave you a fright too. Staying here this evening?' he asks.

'Oh, you didn't frighten me honest. Yes, I'm staying but I'm not supposed to be in this area, Auntie says it's hired out for the night. I'll leave you to your ghost hunting,' I say, trying desperately not to offend them with a laugh that was about to burst out of my mouth.

'That's alright, love. Although we did think we had the capture of the century then,' the dad laughs.

'Yeah,' says William, 'I think it would've broken YouTube.'

'Oh, I'm so sorry. I'll best be getting back now. Goodnight.'

As I'm on my way back to my room I hear it again, 'Uhm.' As though someone is clearing their throat. I take another look around the room and wonder if it's just the radiator acting up. They *are* ancient. I pay it no more attention and hop into bed snuggled under all the warm blankets with Pluto purring by my side.

Chapter Three

A loud purr by my ears rouses me from my slumber. 'Pluto, go and ask auntie for your breakfast,' I murmur, and then slowly open my eyes and take in my surroundings. The air is icy cold and a weak sunbeam pools in from the thin curtains across the floor. My eyes follow the light and for a brief second, I swear I see an outline of a person backed against the wall. I sit bolt upright and clutch Pluto to my chest, but after rubbing the sleep out of my eyes and focusing on the wall again there's nothing. *Stupid imagination!* The problem with all this ghost malarkey is the power of suggestion. I *know* there are ghosts here, well, by that I mean I have been told there is, so of course I'm going to think I'm seeing things. Time to get my scientific brain in gear again.

After texting mum a good morning and telling her that I met a couple of ghost hunters last night by accident, I head downstairs to the kitchen where Auntie is standing at the stove making breakfast.

'How did you sleep, Wend?' asks my aunt as she flips eggs over in the pan. She quickly flips the bacon that's burning and places it on to a plate.

'Like a log,' I reply. I didn't want to tell her I was up walking about and got mistaken for a ghost because I know she would laugh her head off.

'Morning,' I hear from the adjoining dining room. I look back and see William at the table with his dad. Now I can see him in daylight, he's about my age with dark, unruly hair and ice-blue eyes. His dad is pretty much the older version except for stubble and tattoos.

'Morning,' I say, and he waves me over to the table.

'Wend, take that to the Smiths, please,' asks aunt, sounding already flustered and tired. She shouldn't ought to be as she went to bed at the same time.

She hands me two plates full of bacon, eggs, and toast. I turn into the dining area and for some reason William and his dad are staring, open mouth at the laptop screen.

'Breakfast is served,' I say and place the plates on the table.

'Oh, hi there,' William finally clocks on to my presence. 'Sorry about last night. You did give us a fright though.'

'And I'm sorry for disturbing your investigation. So, what's so interesting?' I nod to the laptop.

William nudges his dad. 'Can Wendy have a look?'

'Of course,' he turns the laptop around, so the screen is facing me.

'What am I looking at?'

'This is what we captured last night,' William says excitedly.

'Captured?'

'Ghosts, you know...'

'If you look here,' his dad points at the frozen screen which he slowly rewinds to where a white ball of light shoots out of the darkness across the camera and disappears.

'A dust mote,' I say deadpan.

William's scrunches his eyes at the screen. 'A dust mote? Are you joking?'

'As a matter of fact, no. It's the only logical explanation.'

'Forget logical. That's an orb,' he exclaims. 'It's the beginnings of a ghost manifestation.' He looks incredulous. I want to laugh but thought it was improper and may cost auntie some returning custom she desperately needs. Though, to be honest, it isn't the paranormal she needs, more like a lottery win to fix this place. A rollover if possible.

'A ghost? Right, okay. That's your opinion, I guess, and I respect that, but I believe it's a dust mote. Trust me, the house probably hasn't had a proper clean since 1980.' I look back over my shoulder to ensure auntie wasn't in ear shot of that comment.

'You don't believe in the paranormal, do you?' He asks with a mouthful of eggs.

'No,' I'm disgusted by his eating habits. 'I'm a scientist actually.'

'Are you?' he asks, genuinely interested which surprises me considering I pretty much insulted his hobby.

'Yes, I want to be an astrophysicist.'

'That sounds well cool. Hey, maybe you could join us this evening and give your scientific opinion on what we capture. It will go down well with our YouTube viewers won't it, Dad?'

'Yes, you're more than welcome,' says his dad. 'It will make a great live stream. But ask your aunt for permission first okay.'

'Okay, thank you. I'll leave you to your breakfast then.'

'Catch you later, Wendy.'

'So, what are you getting up to today?' Auntie asks, slicing me a burnt bacon sandwich.

'Not much. Maybe I'll just look around the place and oh, I've been asked if I could take part in a paranormal investigation tonight...'

Auntie laughs. 'You've changed your mind quickly, didn't you? Did you see anything last night?' she asks, now serious.

'No and no, William and his dad asks if I could give my scientific opinion and I need your permission because it will be filmed live.'

'Oh, in that case, I don't see why not. Let me know if anything happens.' She says just like mum and went to wash the dishes.

I hear a rattle and turn to the shelf to see the bottle slightly move. Odd. I have no firm answer to why this has happened, the only thing I can conclude is that it may had been tremors in the Earth. Geophysical, perhaps? Yes, geophysical. And then I clear my plate and head back to my room.

The corridor from the dining room to the main living area and library is lit with candles on the sideboards that has many gold and silver gilded framed pictures of family. I recognise some of the faces from stories mum told me, which has been few and far between over the years, but there's a new picture added since my last visit and it's of a beautiful woman with dark hair and green eyes. She's wearing an ARP uniform which means Air Raid Precautions, so this was definitely taken during the Second World War. But who is she? I must remember to ask Auntie later.

As I walk through the hall, I feel the temperature drop on my right side and a chill trickling down my arm as if water had dripped from the ceiling and was turning frozen like ice. I let out an involuntarily shiver. 'Brr, it's so cold in here, Pluto,' I say as she saunters down the stairs miaowing. She arches her back and looks directly into the living room and then at me. 'Come on, girl,' I say and enter the room, looking at her oddly. She never does this. Aunt's living room should be in a museum. It's like a time capsule back to the 1940s. The fire is roaring, so at least there is some heat in this old place. Tempted by the lure of the heat, I went to stand in front of the fire to take away the sudden chill. But it persisted. It didn't go away. My left side is still cold.

'Stay where you are,' I hear William say behind me.

'Huh?' I turn around and see him standing in the doorway with his laptop. 'Don't move.'

'What are you doing?' I ask.

'There's someone standing to your left,' he says.

'And how would you know that? See,' I wave my arms about to point out the obvious. 'It's just empty space.'

'Not according to this. It maps out figures we can't see with our eyes. There's definitely someone there.'

'Supposing there is. What do we do? Ask if they want a cup of tea?'

'We can use a spirit box to communicate but Dad has it. Maybe we could try later.'

'Alright,' I say, not convinced. 'Ghosts are impossible, you know. There's no such thing.'

'That's your opinion, and I respect it,' he smiles cheekily. His eyes dart towards the bookshelves. 'Wow, there's a lot of books.'

'Yep. My great-aunt was a doctor, or so I believe.'

'Or so you believe?'

'I don't know much about my family to be honest.' I rub my arm for warmth and looked to my side. *What if...? Nah, Wendy, get a grip.*

'That's odd,' he says, and I agree. 'Maybe it's time to ask questions?'

'Maybe I can find out during my stay.'

'I'd love to help.'

'Would you?'

'Yeah, it would be fun. Oh, I must go and help Dad. I'll catch you later,' he was about to turn when something caught his eye. 'I swear I saw... Nah. See you later, Wend.'

When he left the room, I look to my side where he thought he saw something and felt all shivery. Perhaps this was fear? I don't know, but I knew ghosts were impossible and there...

'Ahem.'

'Who's there?' I straighten my shoulders and command: 'Show yourself. You're not a ghost, you're probably some kid having a laugh. I'm not stupid, you know. I'm going to be an astrophysicist.'

A thud of something hitting the floor behind make me jump. I look down and there's a book in front of my feet. I pick it up and blow off years' worth of dust.

'The Diary of Elisa Witchspell.'

Chapter Four

'How convenient,' I mutter, sitting out the front garden on the bench, tapping my fingers on the cover. 'Of all the books to fall on the floor it had to be this one.' I suppose in some way I'm meant to have found it.

'What have you got there?' came a voice but when I look around, I don't see anyone. As I was about to get mad at whoever it was teasing me, an empty crisp packet lands on my head and I look up and see William poking his head out of the window.

'This fell off the bookshelf after you left. It's about my family.'

'Is it? Wow. I'll be down in a sec.' He went back inside and closes the window.

Tomorrow is Halloween and my aunt had a party planned of some sort, so she was busy putting up plastic skeletons in the front garden and gravestones made from foam. I should ask her about the book, but I feel like I need to keep it quiet for a while. Her and mum already have a secret they're hiding and don't want me to know about it, so she may just take the book, who knows?

'What is she doing?' asks William who just appears in front of me.

I look at aunty and there she is stringing lights around the ribcages humming merrily to herself as if this were the most normal thing in the world.

I puff out my cheeks and shake my head. 'I have no idea. I sometimes wonder if we're actually related.'

William sits down on the bench. 'So, let's see what the book says then.'

'Should I?'

'Why not? You have a right to know your family history. Go on.'

'Maybe I shouldn't open it here.'

'Well to be honest it can't be much of a secret if the book was left on the shelf for anyone to read.'

'Yes, that's true but considering the mess I doubt she even knew it was there. Come on, I know just the place.'

We walk around the small car park area to the back door.

'Woah the maze is so cool!' William shrieked. 'What if we can't find our way out though?'

'We will, come on...'

'Oh yeah, I meant to say that dad isn't feeling too well. He went for a walk early this morning and some woman by the shops offered him a sample of some berries you have here. He's been spewing ever since, so I'll have to do the live tonight by myself. Are you still joining me?'

'Oh really, that's unfortunate. Maybe they just didn't agree with him. But, yeah, why not? I'm looking forward to it. It'll be a new experience for sure.'

Walking into the maze it suddenly felt very cold. 'It's freezing all of a sudden,' I say.

'It is too. Weird.'

'So come on then, open it,' William urges.

'Okay...so,' I flip through the book and an envelope falls out and lands by my feet.

'Oh, what's this then?' William stoops down to pick it up and notices two photographs peeking out. He hands them to me. I stare at the black and white picture of the same woman I saw in the hallway. She's standing next to a young man in the fields behind the house. I flip the photo over and it says, *"Hans and Elisa 1942"*. 'Hans? Isn't that a foreign name?'

'German, I think. Are they relatives of yours?' he asks.

'I have no idea,' I shrug. 'I don't know much about my family beyond my grandparents.'

'Only one way to find out then.' He points to the house. 'You've got to ask your aunt.'

I bite my lip. 'I should, shouldn't I?'

When we made it back to the front door, Aunty had text to say she had popped to the shops and wouldn't be long. I resist the temptation to ask her, so go inside the house, to the kitchen. 'Want a snack?' I ask William who I thought was walking beside me. 'William? Where are you?' I turn around and he's standing stock still with his mouth hanging open in the hall facing the library door. 'Do you see him?' he eventually says. 'There,' he points with a quivering finger.

I take a gander at the door and see nothing *but* the door. 'See who?'

He swallows before saying: 'Hans.'

Chapter Five

'Hans?' I blink, staring at the door. 'It's just empty space, William.' I stomp towards the door and wave my arms around to make a point and then stomp back towards the kitchen.

William backs up towards me and clutches my arm. 'He was just there, the man from the photograph. I swear on it, Wendy.'

'Nope, I don't see anything,' I say wondering if he's feeling okay. Maybe it's all the excitement at finding the diary and photos?

'We've got to dig deeper into this. Who is Hans and what is he to Elisa. More importantly who is Elisa to you?'

True enough, I thought. I had to get to the bottom of this story I could feel emerging. 'You're right, I need to do some digging.' I wave the diary around. 'Maybe this will hold some clues.'

We head into the kitchen and sit down at the table. William pours us two mugs of hot chocolate Aunt has left on the stove and then we hover over the brown tattered book. 'So,' I flip over the front cover and begin to read the legible scrawl on now yellowing paper. 'February 10th, 1941. I have just returned from my shift at the local tin factory absolutely exhausted, but I promised Owen I'd take the ARP duty tonight as he had a date with a local girl. So far on my shifts it has been awfully quiet; just the odd, 'turn your lights out,' and that's it. I walk around the village in the pitch black and then return home before daybreak...'

'Elisa's the ARP warden then,' William states the obvious. 'Carry on...'

'It means I was right about the picture in the hall too.' I carry on reading...

'Life in the Black Mountains is very uninteresting. I often wish I could work in places like Bletchley Park and become a spy like my friend, Anne, but I have ties here and a reasonable job, so I can't complain.'

Just then I hear a loud boom and the echo of the front door opening and closing. 'Are you here, Wend?' shouts Auntie.

'Yeah, in the kitchen,' I say.

Auntie strolls into the kitchen with a couple of bags of shopping and pauses to look at the book I'm holding. 'You've found Elisa's diary?' she says, not in the least surprised. 'I was going to talk to you about this actually.' She puts the bags on the countertop, takes out a bar of chocolate and hands it to me. 'A treat...share it with William,' she says and takes a seat at the table. She tucks a lock of hair behind her ear and pulls the book towards her. 'She was my great-aunt, my grandmother's sister, so she'd be your great-great-aunt. Until recently, well, since my grandmother's passing, we weren't allowed to speak of her...'

'Really?' I say, flabbergasted at this revelation. Now I'm beginning to understand mum's reluctance to talk of the family's history. 'But why? What happened?'

'She fell in love with a German.'

'Is that all?' asks William, breaking off his share of the chocolate.

Auntie laughs at his comment. 'Well, during World War Two when the German's were our enemy, it wasn't particularly an ideal situation.'

'So, she was shunned?'

'By the family and the neighbours. You see, Hans, that's her beau, was a pilot and one evening his plane came down in the neighbouring fields. Elisa had been on duty that night and saw it happen. As the story goes, she saved his life and he vowed to repay her for this, but instead of being sent back to his own country, he was detained in a working farm not far from here. Elisa used to visit him often and that's how they fell in love...'

'So, he wasn't a bad German, then?' asks William, chewing on his chocolate obviously rapt in the story.

'Elisa didn't think so, no. He was nineteen-years-old, like Elisa. Most of them at that age didn't want to fight for a cause they didn't support.'

'Is he still hanging around here?' William gets straight to the point.

'That's another thing...Halloween 1944 he was about to be returned in exchange for British prisoners of war, when his plane went down over the ocean...they never recovered the body.'

'And Elisa?'

'Never got over him. And great-granny never forgave her, so the house wasn't passed to her. It was given to my grandad who passed it onto my dad and then me because your mother didn't want it.'

'That's sad.'

'Yeah, really sad,' William says. 'I think I saw Hans by the library,' he says so flippantly you'd swear it was a regular occurrence with him. Then again, he does run a ghost hunting channel.

'It wouldn't surprise me,' Auntie replies. 'It's the anniversary of his death tomorrow.'

William and I both exchange a glance. 'What about Elisa? What happened to her?'

'She passed away just a day before you were born, Wend. In this house. My grandad said she could live out the rest of her days here, so when she passed, I took it over and opened it up as a hotel at first but I couldn't get enough punters in, so then the idea to use it as a ghost hunting venue came to me after I was hearing so many guests complain they were seeing things move on their own. I had to do it because it's in such disrepair and I need the income.'

'Wow what a story!' William exclaims. 'But I did see his ghost just earlier, you know.'

'Perhaps you did. I had one investigator say that Hans was looking for Elisa's spirit but there had been curse put on them both back in the forties by a woman I believe is a relative of ours, but I don't know the full story, if I'm honest. That's why I always make Halloween special here. So, they feel welcome.'

'That's what the article said on the internet, but surely, it's just a legend? What kind of a person can perform curses and make them work?'

Auntie shrugs her shoulders and stands up. 'Maybe that's something you can look into whilst you're here, eh?' she smiles, gets up off the chair and leaves the room.

Chapter Six

'A curse? Now it's getting even more interesting.' William exclaims, heading up the stairs. 'I'm thinking of going out for a walk, fancy coming?' he asks, and I'm sure he's up to something.

'Yeah, why not, I'll grab my coat and a brolly.'

'Okay, meet you outside in five minutes.'

I pull on my raincoat and stand by the open door watching the rain lash down from the grey clouds to the concrete. The idea of walking in this is absurd but it's a breather from the heaviness I've been feeling in the house since William supposedly saw Hans. I can't explain what it is, but I've been feeling as gloomy as the weather ever since.

'Here I am, let's go,' William threw his hood over his head and pulls out his mobile. 'I thought we could go and see the site of the crash,' he suggests. 'It's a fair walk mind but according to this map here there's a footpath at the edge of the woods that leads almost to it.'

'Sounds good,' I say opening the brolly as we take a left on the main road. The road is so narrow there's no pavement so when a car zooms by we squeeze against the hedges taking extra special care that our feet are tucked in as well. Three cars later and a tractor, we keep walking through the tiny village of pretty stone cottages until we stumble upon the opening of the woods. Tall ancient oaks loom above us as we tread through the dirt lined path that is quickly forming to mud under my feet.

'So, have you and your dad been doing paranormal investigations for long?' I ask while I'm taking in my surroundings. The air smells of damp wooden chips and the raindrops bounce off the leaves onto my hood making an annoying patting sound in my ears.

'About a year. We got into it after my mother died. I think it's dad's way of coping with the grief to be honest and I don't mind it, it's fascinating.'

'Oh, I'm sorry to hear about your mum. I think I can understand why he's interested in it, but I'm not sure if I believe in life after death or ghosts for that matter. But this whole thing with Elisa and Hans is weird though.'

'Yeah, if they're supposedly trapped it would be nice to set them free, wouldn't it? I mean, you don't have to believe in the afterlife to help. Just think what if there is one and you have the opportunity to help two spirits finally be together and free from the big old house. It'd be a nice thing to do.'

'I guess that's one way of looking at it,' I reply, still unconvinced spirits lurk on the Earth plane after death. It just defies all my scientific belief and knowledge. 'Are we there yet?' I ask with a nod to his mobile.

'Patience, patience,' he laughs. 'It should be...' he looks up from his mobile gaging a sense of direction. 'Well, it looks like it's just a few feet away...' he turns on his heel, 'down there,' he points. As he points down an embankment forming into a cluster of trees, a small run down looking wooden cottage peeks out between two tree trunks at the very bottom.

'I wonder what that is?' I say. 'Shall we go and look?'

He shrugs. 'Why not? We've come this far. I don't know what we're expecting to find, I mean, the crash was almost eighty years ago. Come on then...' he sets off down the small embankment and turns back to me. 'Is the scientist afraid?' he jokes.

'No, I'm coming,' I say and almost slip on wet leaves. I grab onto a tree to stop myself from falling then regain my balance. I catch up with William and we slowly approach the cottage.

'Okay, so where did the plane come down then?' I ask.

'Can't you see?' He points to the side of the house where there is noticeable gap in trees at the side of the cottage. 'It's there, that's where it crashed. Took down the trees.'

'Oh yeah,' I say, thinking I ought to have figured that out for myself. 'So, what else does the article say on the internet?'

'Um... oh no, I've lost the signal,' he holds up his phone. 'I suppose we should just have a snoop around, see if we can spot something unusual... I don't know to be honest.'

'If there was a curse, who do you suppose set it?' I ask, pondering what Auntie had said.

'No idea,' he says, head down to the ground looking for who knows what.

I decide to join him and look around too, but there was nothing on the ground, and nothing to suggest a war plane had come down here decades ago either. It was then I heard a squelch in the mud and notice at that precise moment neither of us had moved our feet. 'Who's that?' I whisper to William whose eyes had become large with fear also.

'I don't know,' he whispers and make eyes at me as if to say "behind us". With trepidation we both look at each and silently agree to turn around together, and as we do a figure in black is standing before us.

Chapter Seven

'What are you doing here, children?' the woman asks. 'This is private property.'

At this moment in time my eyes are still fixed on her feet, and I'm petrified to look up for fear of what I'd see. I turn to William who is standing rigid to the spot with his mobile in his shaking hand. Finally, I find the courage to raise my head and look and what I see I think has just fallen out of a novel my mother would write.

'We're not doing anything,' William replies meekly. All his bravado just earlier now diminished by the presence of a tall, thin woman dressed in a black dress and cloak with the hood pulled over her head. Her long dark hair flows over and past her shoulders and her features are drawn and pale. She doesn't look that old, probably about Auntie's age. But it's her light blue eyes that are freaking me out because it's as if they can see beyond everything and through me. Gosh she may even know what I'm thinking. Even though I know it's an irrational thought.

'We... we just came to see the site of the crash. We'll be going now.' I tug at William's arm to get moving, but it's almost as if he's transfixed by her presence. 'William, say goodbye to the nice lady and we can go home.'

'Home?' The woman says. 'And where that might be?'

'Just over there,' I point to nowhere in particular.

'The manor house?' she asks, and as she says it her eyes lit up even more.

'No, just...over there. Come on William, we'll be late for tea.'

It takes several tugs to bring him around and finally we leg it back up the embankment and down the path as fast as our feet allow for the slippery mud.

'What was that?' Williams exclaims when we reach the entrance.

'I don't know, but there was an odd presence about her.'

'She looks like a witch, you know, like the ones we read in books when we were kids.'

'We're still technically kids, William.'

'Yeah, but I stopped reading fairytales years ago...you don't still read them, do you?' he smirks.

'No!'

He laughs. It's obvious he doesn't believe me.

'My mother writes books,' I explain. 'Paranormal stuff mainly and that... woman or whatever she is, reminded me of something I read that's all.'

'Your mother writes? Woah that's so cool.'

'Yeah, I guess. Come on, we should get out of here,' I say and head back onto the road to the house.

'WHERE HAVE YOU TWO been? You're like drowned rats,' Auntie says. 'Go on, get changed because dinner is almost ready. And William, your dad is still a bit sick, so I said you can eat with us is that alright?'

'That's brilliant, thanks. I'll just go check on him. See you in a bit, Wendy.'

'What are you standing there for, Wend, go and get changed before you get sick. Go on, shoo!' She flicks her hand and heads back into the kitchen where the smell of a lasagne wafts into the hallway. Auntie has always been the better cook out of her and mum, but I'd never tell mum that.

When I get to my room, Pluto sits up and toddles over to me, brushing his head against my leg. 'Nice to see you too,' I say and get out my phone to text mum. I just have to ask her about a book she wrote because something about the woman in the woods was feeling familiar.

Mum, what was that book you wrote that had a witch in it that lived in the woods? So cliché but it worked.

While I'm waiting for her to answer I begin to get changed for dinner. Remembering the paranormal investigation tonight and the fact that I was going to be live on YouTube I get out my new black and red stripey jumper from my case. Then there was a ping on my phone.

Thanks, Wend, I love it when you're kind about my books. Joking. I know you keep me on my toes. It's the one I wrote for you when you were six, remember? The Witches Curse. I can send you it over if you want to read it again or...

Or what?'

Well, I wondered if there's a reason for you asking for it that's all.

Why would there be a reason?

Well... have you figured it out yet? I suppose I should've realised how intelligent you are and that it wouldn't take you long.

Mum… just be honest, please…

The Witch's Curse is sort of based on a real story. Wilhelmina was right, I should've told you a long time ago. As strange as it may sound to you, many years ago, back in 1941 I believe, a German airplane crashed in the woods. The story goes that Elisa was on ARP duty that day and saw it come down. Knowing the pilot was close to death, and being the kind woman she was, she begged someone who supposedly had healing abilities to help bring him from the brink but nobody really knows what she had to exchange for it, but it's said Elisa and Hans, her love, are roaming the old house because of this silly curse and can't move on from there until it's broken.

That makes sense then… I'll speak to you later.

Let me know if you find out anything because if anyone does, it'll be you, I know it.

I say goodbye to mum and tell her I'll keep her up to date with my findings and turns to head back downstairs for dinner when the bedroom door opens and then slams right in front of my eyes. *On its own!* Probably a draught, I think and as I reach out to open it, an icy cold chill settle on my hand and I pull it away immediately. I don't know what to think at this precise moment, and then Pluto leaps from the bed miaowing like crazy at nothing in particular.

'What is it?' As I approach her, she begins to hiss and then roll on the bed purring as though someone was smoothing her. I back out of the room and run downstairs, bumping into William about to make his way to dining room.

'What's up with you?' he asks.

'Okay, I admit it. Something weird is going on here I don't have an explanation for.'

William grins. 'I was hoping you'd come around.'

'That does not mean I believe in ghosts. I'm just saying things are happening here that are...well, a little out of the ordinary. Let's leave it at that.'

Okay,' he says, as we take our seats at the table. 'I bet by the time I go home you will be a true believer,' he grins and then stuffs a forkful of lasagne into his mouth.

'We shall see,' I smile knowing very well I wouldn't be.

Chapter Eight

Standing on the landing where I first saw William and his dad, I involuntarily shiver at the sub-zero temperature it has going on whilst waiting for William to set up the camera tripod. We've already set up cameras in the other rooms so that he can get extra footage for another episode.

'We're going live in about twenty minutes,' he says and then checking his laptop. '567 people are waiting already,' he exclaims. 'I don't think we've had that many waiting before. Are you nervous?'

I had no idea they were so popular and now the realisation that I'll be on camera suddenly hits me, but I can't say no now, can I? 'Nah, I didn't know you had a big following.'

'Twenty-four thousand. Surprising, isn't it considering we've only been doing this about six months.'

'No pressure then.'

William laughs. 'No pressure, Wendy, it's the ghosts that does the work, not us.'

'But what if you don't capture anything?' I offer even though I knew the likelihood of anything appearing on camera or even in front of my eyes were minimal possibly even smaller than an atom.

'We don't always get anything and that's what makes our videos authentic because people know then we don't fake anything. We can't just conjure a ghost out of a hat, that would be stupid.'

Stupid, indeed.

'Right,' he gets to his feet and hands me a small camera. 'You'll be using this camera too so we can get extra footage for our patron's page. So, basically just follow me and make comments on things we see, such as that thing,' he points to a small box on the floor. 'If that lights up, it usually means that an unseen force is touching it.' He goes over to it and proves it by waving his hand around it. 'It doesn't go off, but if I touch the wire...' The box suddenly lit up blue. 'That means it's being touched by an entity.'

'Right... I see.'

'So, your job tonight is to discount anything you see.'

That shouldn't be too difficult then. 'I get it.' At this point I'm starting to sweat. I can't believe I agreed to this.

'Just act natural, pretend the cameras aren't there,' he says noticing my nervousness.

I want to say 'yeah' but nothing comes out of my mouth. William laughs and then checks the time on his phone. 'Five minutes. I just want to make sure all the cameras are on, won't be a tick,' he goes off to the other rooms whilst I stand in the corridor with the camera in hand. This will be a breeze; I convince myself when I notice the light flashing on the REM pod. 'Uh, Will, is this thing meant to go off?' He ducks his head out of the door.

'Er, did you touch it?' he asks.

'No.'

'Well then, no not unless...'

'Ghosts?' I offer.

'You're coming round to the idea, aren't you?' He does that smirk again, but I know he's joking. 'Looks like stuff is starting already, come on then, let's go live. Once I do the introductions, the lights go out.'

I nod, feeling a slight tightness in my chest. Come on, Wendy, you can do this!

'Five... four... three... two... Hi guys, welcome to The Ghost Crew. We have a special show for you tonight, and a special guest, but first things first, Mr S can't be with us this evening because he's currently sick in bed...Oh, I can see all your comments coming in now... Thanks for your well wishes, I'm sure he's reading them as I speak... Anyway, before I announce where we are, our special guest this evening is Wendy whose aunt owns the property we are investigating. Say hi, Wendy...'

'Hi everyone.' I wave, feeling my cheeks get hot.

'Wendy is a scientist and I thought it'd be a great idea if Wendy could follow us around this evening and give her scientific views on what we'd find...so without further ado, we're in Witchspell Manor, yes, it's been requested a lot and we finally booked it for a two-part Halloween special.' He continues to talk into the camera.

It's almost dark outside and the shadows are drawing closer. Whether it's all that I've heard about witches and curses or the atmosphere that has been created, I'm beginning to feel apprehensive. I hold the camera towards William and then follow him as he walks down the corridor, into the blackness.

'Is there anyone here who would like to communicate with us?' he says and pulls out his phone. 'I'm currently using the spirit talking App that Mr S created. If you want to download this, it's free until the 31st...'

Spirit talking app? We're standing outside one of the rooms and goes to enter when a voice comes over the phone. 'Help, we're stuck.'

Both me and William stop in our tracks. I keep the camera on the phone and stare at William. 'It's probably interference, you know, radio signals perhaps...'

He raises a brow and seems unconvinced with my explanation. 'Remember the story?' He says, and then goes on to explain to the audience all that we've uncovered over the last day. When I hear it aloud, it sounds like the beginnings of a story my mother would tell, except the ending hasn't been written yet. Truthfully, I'm a little weary since we've encountered the 'witch' in the woods. Talk about cliché though!

We step into the room that's in pitch darkness, and with only the night vision to see my way I follow William while he's answering questions coming in on the live chat. It seems like everyone is excited over the witch and the mystery surrounding the manor. Most are feeling sorry for Hans and Elisa's spirits. I must admit, I am too. I suppose if there's a way I can help, I will. I pan the camera around, looking through the lens when a dark shadow, blacker than the darkness we're in zooms across the lens. Stepping back, I bump into a cupboard of sorts when William whips the camera on me.

'What's happened?' he asks.

'Well,' I say, suddenly gaining more confidence. 'I think it may have been an insect or something passing across the camera lens to the door...'

'Like a shadow?' he asks.

'Sort of...'

'Cool...'

With that, a loud crash from across the room makes us both jump out of our skin. 'What was that?' I ask, making my way to the source of the noise when to my horror I see a figure of a man sitting in a chair.

Chapter Nine

'It's Hans!' Screeches William.

I blink and he's gone - if it was even him. 'I think we're a little over simulated tonight what with everything, and that's probably why we think we're seeing things,' I suggest before he actually says it's his spirit, but it's too late. He's absolutely convinced, and people are writing in the comments that they saw him too.

'Guys, I think we're going to call it a night,' he says. 'But tomorrow is the big Halloween special, so tune in for that because if tonight is anything to go by it will be a blast! Let me know if you've seen or heard anything we didn't.' He ends the live, switches on his torch and turns to me. 'Wendy, I'm telling you it was him...'

'It was...' came a voice from behind us.

I can't move. I can't even open my mouth to scream. For once, I have no explanation for what I'm hearing and I'm dreading to turn around. William nudges me and urges me to look. Do I dare? *Oh, come on, Wendy, you're a scientist, there's probably a logical explanation for it.* William pans the torch towards the door, and a full-bodied figure of a man with blond hair is staring at us, not frighteningly, but seemingly desperate for help. Almost pleading with the lightest blue eyes, I have ever seen. But there's something odd about him because I can see clearly through him unless he's wearing the door.

'Don't be scared,' he says and now I can pick out a German accent. 'I don't have much time to communicate with you, it takes a lot of energy for one but there's also a curse on my spirit...'

'You're a... Oh my god, I'm having an hallucination!' I say.

'If so then I'm having the same one and tell me, Wendy, is that scientifically possible?'

'I don't have much time,' Hans chimes in. 'There's a curse and it needs to be undone before midnight tomorrow. I really need your help.'

William nods, mouth agape. I don't even know what's going on right now, but I know what I'm seeing but part of me don't want to believe it.

'What do you need us to do?' I find myself asking.

'Elisa made a pack with a witch many years ago and she bound us to the manor, only Elisa's spirit is contained in another part of the building I can't reach. I don't even know exactly where she is, but I remember the day she passed away and saw her spirit for a brief moment before she vanished. You need to break the curse to set us freeee...' and with that, he disappeared right before my very eyes.

William slams on the light switch and if I wasn't so sure he was actually alive I'd swear he too was also a ghost. His face was as white as a sheet and that, whatever I had seen was not the usual ghost I would come to expect. He wasn't wearing a white sheet, he looked as though he was human but... slightly opaque. Okay, my brain is confuddled.

'We've just witnessed an intelligent apparition!' He breathes and a bit of colour pops back on his cheeks. Thankfully, as I was getting worried.

'I... I just don't know...'

'Wendy! It was a spirit. It's Hans. Your great auntie's fiancé. He spoke to us, and he wants our help.'

'But...'

'We promised we'd help if we could, didn't we?'

I nod, feeling slightly dizzy. For once, I can't explain that I just can't. If I had been the only one who saw him, then maybe I could pass it off as a figment of my imagination... or something, although there's nothing wrong with me...oh what am I saying? We both saw him and that's that. Accept it, Wendy. You saw a ghost!

'Where do we even start?' I ask.

'Maybe Elisa's diary and if I'm not mistaken that strange woman, we saw today has something to do with this.'

'You think?' I say as we head out of the room and down the corridor to the stairs.

'Absolutely. She was curious where we were from, and did you notice her face when she mentioned the manor house?'

'I did to be honest. It was odd.'

Chapter Ten

Sitting at the kitchen table with chocolate, sweets, and doughnuts spread out before us like a medieval banquet, I open Elisa's diary whilst stuffing a chocolate éclair which was no doubt for auntie's Halloween party tomorrow. The pages are yellowing with age and so thin, I take care not to rip them. William is leaning over the books with his camera still rolling.

'I think it'd be a great idea if we record everything from now on,' he says, and I agree. Written in cursive writing is an entry from 1941. I read aloud:

'I wish the family had never made an outcast of the old witch; she surely is a wicked witch if there ever was one. How she has lasted this long is beyond me. It's not natural, even by our standards. But Hans... My dear Hans. If people could see his gentle side; he is not at all like they make them out to be. Betty seems to have it in for me, I am sure of it because why else would she make such a deal with me?'

Both William and I exchange shocked glances. 'Whoa,' William whistles, 'This is getting interesting, isn't it?'

'It goes to show how much I know about my family,' I say, 'which is absolutely nothing after reading this.'

William nods whilst stuffing a spoonful of ice-cream in his mouth. 'Betty... I wonder if she's the woman in the woods?'

I think for a moment, remembering the woman's features, though menacing at first glance because most likely we were on her property, she wasn't that old, so it is impossible that she is the Betty mentioned in the diary but then again...

'No, she can't be. She'd be about ninety-years-old now and unless she has found the fountain of youth, it's not her. She's way too young.'

As we sit and discuss our thoughts, a rattling noise coming from the shelf behind us has us swinging around in our chairs, and just as William pans the camera on it, a bottle slips off and falls to the floor smashing into a sea of green glass.

'Oops,' he says, and turns to me. 'How did that happen? Did you bump the wall with the chair or something?'

I get up off the chair and kneels to inspect the broken pieces. 'No. This happened earlier, when I arrived, I mean.' I poke around the glass, but nothing appears to have fallen out of it, no liquid, solids, nothing. How strange.

'I hope I captured this on camera. This is classic poltergeist activity.'

'We can't just jump to conclusions; we have to investigate it properly.' I get up off the floor and find a pan and brush in the kitchen sink cupboard and clean the mess before auntie sees it. Thinking back to earlier, she did seem a little protective of the bottles for some odd reason. 'We've got to solve this, and I think the first thing to do is to visit the woods again.'

'I agree. Should we go now?

'I shrug. 'Why not. We need to find out who exactly this woman is and if she has any links to the house or my family.' I open drawers in the kitchen hoping to find another torch. 'Got one,' I hold it up and leave the kitchen to get my coat hanging in the hallway only to find Pluto standing by the door waiting for me. 'How did you know I was going out? Come on then, you may as well come with us.'

We step out into the pitch blackness and make our way to the entrance, keeping the light of the torch shining on the floor as not to alert auntie. I keep glancing skywards for anymore shooting stars and whatever else I may find but try also to stay mindful of the road, except at this hour it's so quiet you could hear a pin drop.

'Supposing she is a real witch?' William switches on his mobile's torch and shines it on Pluto walking ahead of us.

'Really? If anything, she's just a bitter woman who enjoys living on her own.'

'I'm not so sure, Wendy. Even as a scientist you must admit this evening has been a strange one.'

He's right, of course. I don't have an explanation for seeing Hans, well, not yet anyway. 'I wonder where Elisa is though, if there's such a thing as an afterlife.'

'Good question and we need to find them soon I reckon so they can move on.'

'Yeah, but I have a funny feeling it's a bit more complicated and I reckon this curse is going to be a tough one to break.'

We come to a sudden halt on the path leading into the woods. I don't think either of us anticipated how dark and lonesome it would be at this stupid hour. Although, it didn't seem to bother Pluto at all and she saunters ahead of us, occasionally looking back at us as if urging us to follow.

'I have a weird feeling about this,' he says.

Armed with our sources of light that barely made a different to the expanse of the darkness, we set off into the woods.

'I don't know why you're scared,' I say to William. 'You spend enough time in the dark with ghosts as it is.' I chuckle at this just as I hear the tooting of an owl and almost jumps out of my skin.

'Looks like you are too,' he laughs. 'We'll be okay. Think about it this way: if she was going to harm us, she would've chased us out of the woods yesterday, but she didn't.'

'I hadn't thought of that, but it still doesn't give me confidence.'

Pluto trudges on ahead and I wonder where or how she even knows where we're going but Pluto has always been super intelligent and intuitive. Then again, cats are. We're just coming to the cottage, if you can even call it that when William grabs hold of my arm.

'Stop,' he whispers, 'can you hear that?'

Pluto also stops too, turns around and walks back towards us, stopping at my feet. Above the rustling of the trees, I do hear a faint chanting and the smell of smoke. 'I hear something, but I'm sure it's nothing to worry about.'

'What do you mean chanting isn't nothing to worry about? Gosh, you are a strange one, aren't you? Does anything scare you for real? Okay, walk slowly,' he suggests and carries on up the path. We come to a tree at the top of the embankment and stands behind it, peering down onto the cottage.

'Shall we go and knock this time?' I ask, but William puts the torch light onto his face and gives me a 'are your serious look'.

'Okay, we'll just stand here all night then.'

'I don't think we have to,' William points. 'It's already getting interesting.'

Chapter Eleven

To my utter surprise and shock, I stare at the window where a candle is glowing on the windowsill and see my auntie sitting at a table conversing with the 'witch'. 'This can't be right. What's she doing there?' I ask and turn to William who's shaking his head, also in disbelief.

'There's one way to find out but I'm not sure it's a good idea. I mean, we don't know what side of the story they're on. If we're the protagonists, there's got to be an antagonist isn't there?'

'This isn't a novel, William, as much as my mother would love this right now. She's my aunt,' I say indignantly, but even I'm not too sure now remembering the conversation between her and mum. Just then I see them shake hands and get up from the chairs. I back further behind the tree, William too, when the door finally opens. Pluto arches her back and looks up at me. I take this as a sign it's not good.

'Until tomorrow then. I hope the elements will be in our favour.'

'I hope so, too, Wilhelmina, it has been a long time coming for sure.'

'It really has. It ends tomorrow night at the stroke of midnight.'

'Absolutely, we'll see to that.'

Auntie walks to the side of the house and disappears into the expanse of the woods. I let out a breath and urge William away once the 'witch' has gone inside.

'Well, we did find out something, didn't we? So, we should go back in case she finds out I'm missing.'

'Yeah, good point...'

'It's a good point indeed,' came an old cackling voice behind us. Pluto hisses and backs up towards my legs. From the shadows, an elderly woman in black with a hooked nose and wrinkly face is standing in front of us. 'Wilhelmina and Mari were two little tearaways when younger and nothing much has changed since. Goodness knows what they're up to, but I can assure it isn't good. Best stay out of their way, you'll only end up the worst for it.'

'Who are you and what do you want?'

'Now, now children,' she says, condescendingly. 'There's no need for the rudeness. Maybe I can be of help... Follow me if you be so kind.'

'Why should we trust you?'

'You want to know about the Witchspell family, don't you?'

William pats his coat and I know he's telling me he has the camera still recording. 'How do you know what we're looking for?'

'Because there's only one reason you're hanging around that cottage. I saw you yesterday too. A cup of hot chocolate and a warm fire waiting for you if you wish to take me up on the offer. I mean, what can old, defenceless lady do...' She chuckles to herself and sets off down the path.

'I guess she has a point,' William says, shrugging his shoulders. 'Come on, we've got it all on camera anyway.'

We follow her hunched figure in the opposite direction from the path that leads to the entrance, occasionally glancing at each other warily. For an old lady she surely can walk fast and before we know it, we've taken another turn, battled our way through long, thin branches that threatened to scratch our faces, and arrive at a wooden cottage that could've come straight out of Hansel and Gretel.

'Woah,' William whispers. 'You would never think it's here, would you?'

'No, but if fairytales are anything to go by perhaps this isn't a good idea. You know they have a dark side, don't you?'

'Fairytales are for kids and there's nothing here to suggest we're in any danger.'

'Fairytales are definitely NOT for kids. Here you go,' she pushes open the door and we step inside, a fire is roaring and, I'd say conveniently, there's several mugs on the table and a pot steaming on the stove. It's almost as if she was expecting us.

She gestures us to a wooden table, and we pull out some chairs and sits down. 'So how long have you lived here?' I ask.

'For as long as I can remember,' she smiles and sits on a stool by the fire. 'So, you're related to the Witchspells?' she asks.

I nod.

'Yes, you look like a Witchspell. You have inherited the green eyes.'

'Sorry, but who did you say were again?' William asks. 'I don't recall you introducing yourself.'

She pokes the fire with an iron stick and turns to us. 'Oh, I'm sorry my dears, I thought I had.'

'No, you didn't,' I say feeling a knot forming in my stomach. Something just doesn't feel right here but I can't seem to put my finger on it.

'Bertha, just Bertha,' she turns back to the fire and throws on a log. 'I was a friend of the family, but that's another story. So, the Witchspell family... What do you think the name suggests?' she asks.

In all my years I had not once thought anything of my surname. Yes, it's not common but after a few moments thought I said, "witch spell." Is there something in our name?'

'Clever girl, I can see you'll do well when you're older... The Witchspell name derives from the first witch, Morganna, who is your great-great-great-grandmother and yes, my dear, you are descended from a very long line of witches.'

I thought I had seen and heard everything tonight what with Hans' supposed ghost, but this was on another scale of crazy. 'A witch!' I blurts out, laughing. 'Oh, come off it, my mother can't even conjure up a decent spaghetti Bolognese. We're no witches, I'm telling you.'

'Oh, is that what you think? Maybe you need to start asking questions, Wendy Witchspell.'

'How...'

'Oh, I know everything that goes on. Let's say I have ears and eyes everywhere... Now, to the reason I believe you were hanging around Mari's cottage. You know about the curse on Hans and Elisa, don't you?'

'Yes, and I know they're both stuck and want to move on to the...' I clear my throat, 'spirit world.'

Bertha laughs. 'You don't believe, do you? But you,' she points to William. 'You do.'

William nods and I think if he doesn't stop his head will fall off.

'The curse was set on Halloween 1941 when Elisa asked the most powerful witch in the family to spare Hans' life when his plane crashed, but in order to do so, Elisa had to give something in return, something important to her – her soul, which is, I believe is secured in a glass bottle in the house. To set her free one would have to break the curse on Halloween, before midnight and to do so one would have to perform the reversal and it's a no mean feat, I can tell you as it will also involve a sacrifice.'

Glass bottles? Oh, that would explain why Auntie was so worried over them and that would also mean she knows. 'Supposing I believe any of this, where would I get the spell from and what does the sacrifice involve?' I ask and I can't believe I'm going along with this nonsense, but here I am, supposedly descended from a witchy family asking a strange old lady how to do magic. I have to keep reminding myself that I'm a scientist.

'If you bring me the bottle, I may be able to help.'

'Okay, but there are many. How do I know which one it is? Do you know?'

'Of course, it's the blue one with a golden stopper. Bring it to me first thing. Now,' she gets to her feet. 'Off you go, it's late and we don't want Wilhelmina looking for you, do we?' She smiles, and the wrinkles around her green eyes crinkle. I'm not sure if it's with compassion or evil intent because I still can't put my finger on what's wrong here.

Chapter Twelve

Finally, we made it to the main road, still intact, and no harm done. Yet. William quickly pulls his mobile from his pocket where he has been recording all this time and checks the video back.

'This is going to make one fantastic video, I tell you. Talk about viral, this is going to be watched for Halloween's to come!'

We start walking back to the house, and I'm pondering on all I've seen and heard tonight. 'Do I trust my aunt, William?'

'What?' he lifts his head from his phone. 'Oh, your auntie, um, I don't know to be honest. You heard her and that Mari making plans for tomorrow night, didn't you? Maybe we should be cautious that's all and find out what they're up to. It has to involve the ghosts somehow, sure of it.'

'Yeah, I suppose it's not worth mentioning right now, but what of that strange woman. Do you think there was something odd about it all'?

'Nah, at first, I thought it was, but she just seems like a lonely old lady. I wouldn't worry too much. We'll find the bottle and take it to her first thing in the morning.'

'I agree, then hopefully she can set Hans and Elisa free.'

William turns to me, smirking. 'I'm still going to make a believer out of you before Halloween ends,' he says, and we walk into the Manor grounds to the front door just as an owl toots making me jump out of my skin.

As we walk into the hallway, it's in pitch darkness except for the grandfather clock's face that's cast in the moonlight about to struck midnight.

'Wait for it,' I say, and we stand in the freezing cold, watching the hand about to strike twelve, October 31st, Halloween.

'Four... three... two... one...'

DONG! DONG! DONG!

'My god it's loud enough to wake up the dead,' William says, hands covering his ears.

'Maybe it already has,' I say casting the light of the torch on my face and making spooky noises. We both fall about laughing when a passing cloud blocks out the moonlight and suddenly everything becomes silent and still as if it were building up to a dramatic conclusion. Just then I turn to William, and I see a blacker than black shadow coming towards us.

'Run,' I tug his sleeve and finally he sees what I do. We sprint towards the kitchen, slam the door close and dive under the table. The tiles are freezing under the palms of my hands and there's a hint of chocolate in the pan reminding me how hungry I am. But there's no time to think about my empty stomach right now. 'What was that?' I whisper. 'It's blacker than a blackhole!'

'Shadow people,' he says. 'Not good.'

'Huh?'

'No time to explain.'

Peering out of the table at the bottom of the kitchen door, a black mist seems to come through it, then it's followed by footsteps approaching from the hallway.

'What should we do?' I whisper watching the blackness swarm around the door.

'Just stay put,' William advises, and I can see the light of his phone screen filming the whole thing. The footsteps get nearer, and nearer to the door when my breath hitches and it opens, and a light comes on followed by auntie's feet. I press a finger to my lips and decides not to alert her to our presence. She walks to the sink, fills up the kettle and gets herself a mug from the cupboard. Okay, so nothing unusual in this, but where's the shadow gone? She then walks around the table to the shelves.

'Won't be long now, Elisa. We'll soon sort you out,' she chuckles, and I don't know if it's a good chuckle or what! The kettle comes off the boil and she pours the hot water into her mug and leaves the kitchen, only to turn back and switch the light off plunging us into darkness again. I'm beginning to wonder if that old Bertha was right.

'We have to get the bottle now,' I say crawling out of the table on my knees. 'Put the camera light on the shelf, will you?'

Did she say it was golden, or something?'

'A golden topper, yeah but it's blue.'

'There it is,' he points to the end of the shelf.

'Okay, let me get a chair to reach. Where do you suppose we hide it?' I ask, climbing onto the chair and moving several bottles out of the way. The last thing we wanted was any to fall and smash alerting auntie.

'Just keep it in your room 'til the morning and we'll take it to her after breakfast.'

I precariously reach for the bottle and hold it in my hands, noticing a swirling white mist inside. 'This just don't make sense to me,' I utter under my breath. Everything I believe was being put into question and it was making me feel empty and lonely inside.

Chapter Thirteen

Just like when we came in, the hall is in darkness and there's no sign of auntie anywhere. 'What do you suppose that shadow was?' I ask William waving his camera around.

'I don't know, it sort of disappeared when your aunt came in...wait, do you think she conjured it? The old woman said you were from a line of witches, didn't she? Hey, that, makes you a witchy scientist,' he laughs.

'Oh, ha ha. I'm no witch, but my aunt is into dark magic. Is that what you're saying? I don't... actually, I don't really know.'

We walk up the staircase, careful not to make too much noise as the old stairs had seen better days and were squeakier than the mice aunt says she definitely doesn't have but does. As we reach William's floor, he asks for my mobile. 'I'll put my number in it so if you see or hear anything tonight, let me know, alright?'

'Will do. I'll see you at breakfast then,' I say goodnight and head up the stairs to the attic room, pushing open my door warily. I fumble for the lamp, switch it on, and flounce on my bed with a head reeling with a billion thoughts. 'Descended from witches? Auntie is into dark magic... Maybe, who knows? A peculiar woman in the woods... What is going on, Pluto?' I yawn and crash on the bed before I remember I'd better let mum know. No doubt it'll be her next bestseller.

I hop into bed and Pluto comes to snuggle whilst I text mum everything. It's unlikely she'd read it tonight as it's 2 a.m., so I sink into the covers and grab Elisa's diary from the bedstand, hoping she has written something on the family's past.

'Betty's such an incorrigible woman but I did not mean her any harm. Falling into the water like that and drowning is such a horrible way to go, but wishing someone ill fortune isn't magic, is it? Is it? Did I really kill dear old Betty? They found her at the creek in woods this afternoon, by her house after she found out that my father had cut her from his will after he had found out that she had struck a deal with me over Hans. I'm beginning to wonder if my magic 'powers' are really getting stronger by the day, and I caused her most unfortunate death. I just hope not, but I fear her more in death than alive.'

'Oh gosh, this is getting interesting, Pluto, but who is this Betty...'

'Aunt Betty is due to be buried in the woods in which she lived out her years. Father says that she would be most at peace there where he hopes she won't cause any harm in the afterlife...'

I grab my phone and text William.

'You'll never guess what? My 3x great aunt Betty is the one who put the curse on Elisa, and Elisa thinks that she killed Betty after some wishful thinking... We've got to go to the woods now and find her gravestone. Maybe that will hold more clues.'

Several minutes later, William replies:

'Grab your coat! I'll get my camera.'

'This is getting interesting, isn't it?' he says, heading back downstairs and out of nowhere. We hear a voice say: *I don't think it's such a good idea.*

'Who said that?' I ask stopping dead in my tracks to the front door.

'Oh, it's just the stupid ghost app I left running on my phone... Who do you suppose said that?'

'Hans.' It says clear as a bell and intelligently, which meant it understood us.

'Spirits talk through the phone now?' I'm flabbergasted.

'It's an app which they can use to manipulate words... Wow, so Hans is around. Hans if you can hear me what do you know about Betty?'

'Evil.'

A cold chill runs down my back and I'm seriously having second thoughts about going out at this time. This is all too much to even think straight forget logical.

As we traipse the route to the woods again, there is a distinct sound of chanting and just over the shadowy branches of the tree I can see smoke billowing from Mari's cottage. Either it's on fire and she's happy about it hence the chanting or... she's doing a ritual of some kind. I lean towards the latter and ask William if we're nearly there yet.

'It's just down here,' he turns down a bendy path, and with only the light of the mobile to lead the way we hurriedly try to find the cottage, but my foot hits something solid and I stumble and fall, my hands sinking into wed and soggy mud.

'Wend, are you okay?' William rushes to my side and helps me to my feet. He pans the torch where I tripped and there is a small stone half buried in the earth. 'What is that?' I wonder and take a proper look. 'Give me some light,' I ask and when the light shines on it several words carved into the stone chills me to the bone. *'Here lies Bertha.'*

Chapter Fourteen

'Bertha? But... she's...,' I point to where her cottage would be only to see a heap of broken stone.

'Wendy,' William whispers and for some reason I wish he hadn't as it's creeping me out. 'If Betty's supposedly buried here, who do you think Bertha is?'

'I was thinking the same. Betty! Oh my god why didn't I figure this out before.'

'Hans was warning us.'

'Then why didn't he actually tell us?' I shout but didn't really mean to.

'Because this app only has a limited word capacity!'

'Why are we arguing?'

'I don't know but we need to get out of here.'

We get back on the path and sprint to the entrance when a shadow materialises on the floor in front of me. I stop and back up towards William. 'See it?'

'Yeah, it's a shadow, something like we saw in the house, isn't it?'

I nod but I don't think he actually saw it and I'm too stunned right now to speak. The shadow stands before us blocking the path, its dark mass becoming larger and larger, until its almost seven feet tall and glides towards us. Of course, it's gliding because it has no legs as far as I can see... No legs!? A jolt of fear like I have never felt before surges through me. My brain is telling me to run but my feet feel permanently attached the ground as if they're glued.

'William, I can't move!' I yell, as it gets closer and closer, and the overwhelming sense of gloom pervades me again. 'It's really negative, I can feel it.'

'Yeah, I'm not surprised because I think it's Bertha or is it Betty and she's not happy.' He grabs my arm, pulling be back and together we walk backwards up the path whilst keeping an eye on the shadow looming towards us.

'Where is it?' she asks, her voice high and cackly.

'Where's what?' I ask, knowing full well what she means.

'The bottle that's what you cheeky child.'

I don't know what I'm looking at, or what it is or made from, but the image of Bertha before me annoys me so much I shout, 'Don't you dare call me cheeky. I will not be giving you Elisa's spirit, just because you made the most ridiculous arrangement ever with her. I mean, what was even your problem?!'

At that moment, I realise I should've kept my mouth shut because she becomes incensed to the point her form expands more and a black arm reaches out and snatches William.

'Wendy, help!' He screams in her grasp as he rises higher and higher into the air.

'If you want your friend back, get me that bottle...' and then she's gone. And so has William. Only his camera was left on the ground.

I snatch the camera and with a pounding heart I run down the path, hitting stray branches out of my way. After seeing that I realise there's nothing left to fear out here, except for a sudden fluttering of wings bursting forth from a nearby tree made me gasp with shock. Okay, so there's nothing to fear now except fear itself and to be perfectly honest I'm done with it. I had to find a way to get William back without handing over the bottle containing Elisa's spirit. Maybe it was time to think scientifically not metaphysically. Or maybe I could combine the two?

Chapter Fifteen

I'm out of the woods when a gust of wind picks up almost pushing me onwards to the manor. If I wasn't so scientifically inclined, I'd say the elements wanted me back to the manor quick sharp. The road to the manor is in darkness except for a solitary light in the upstairs window of someone's cottage. I resist the urge to ask for help as I was having a difficult enough time swallowing what *I* saw, so imagine explaining any of this to some old dear! Then, out of the darkness I see two glowing eyes sauntering towards me and I'm so grateful for company. 'Pluto,' I yell and on hearing my voice she runs towards me, but as she does, she looks up at the sky as if drawing my attention to something. 'What's up, girl?' I ask and look to the sky. As if this night couldn't get any stranger, there are women riding broomsticks flying overhead into the woods. 'Are you seeing what I'm seeing?' I say, remembering the camera and pressing record. I blink a few times stupidly believing I'm seeing things, but there really is women on broomsticks with pointy hats and all I can keep thinking is that mum's going to have some serious book sales. 'Oh gosh, William!' I sprint to the manor with Pluto in one hand, miaowing like crazy because she's so heavy and slipping out of my arms.

I reach the gate and Pluto takes this opportunity to jump out of my arms, no doubt annoyed at her bumpy ride. I push open the door and stand in the hallway thinking what to do and out of the corner of my eye I see something red flashing in the library. The REM pods! Someone's touching it – maybe! 'Hello? Who's there?' I whisper because I don't really want to wake auntie up at the moment, despite the fact she's family I'm still on the fence where her loyalty lies. 'Hello?' I switch on the light of the camera enabling me to see night vision and locate the pod on the floor beside the fire. 'If anyone is here and want to communicate...' I had to stop for a moment because I feel ridiculous saying it but all that I saw tonight has me questioning things, so I carry on. 'If you can help me, please flash twice...' I wait and a cold gust of wind brushes past my face and then I see two lights flashing. 'Okay, thank you,' I say, keeping calm and respectful because I really don't know what I'm dealing with. 'If you're Hans, can you flash this once?' The pod flashed once. 'Thank you, Hans. Bertha has taken William and there's witches flying into the woods. What do I do right now? Can you help? Flash once, please.' The pod flashed once and as it did, I feel something slip out of my pocket and fall on the floor. My phone is facing upright with the App store open! I shake my head and then realise what I'm supposed to do... The Ghost Talking App!

I download it and before I can begin asking questions it says: Hello Wendy.

'Hello Hans... Can you help?'

'Yes. Bertha evil. Wants to be human again.'

'Wait! What, really?'

'Need Elisa's soul.'

'Oh my gosh! What can I do?'

'Maze... Go.'

'The maze? But what's there?' I ask but no other reply comes through, so I rush out the door still holding the camera and the phone and head around the side of the building to the maze in the back garden. I shine the torch on it and think I have to go through it but what for? I trudge slowly across the lawn and stand at the entrance to the maze. Who built it and for what purpose I don't know but they always creep me out especially in stories mum use to read to me... Oh my God, the story! The Witch's Curse! Mum is guiding me all the way, I'm sure of it. I set the camera down on the floor and open my phone to find the digital version of mum's story when I notice pinkish and yellow streaks above the mountains. Daybreak is here and I sigh with relief the night has passed, but William is still missing, and I don't have time to stand around. I scroll through the story and find the part on the maze.

'Daisy could feel the temperature drop dramatically and the only place she knew she'd be safe was in the maze, yes, the dreaded maze she had feared since she was a child. Inside, she knew the secret to the capturing the witch and ending the curse lay at the very centre because it is believed that once a bad witch entered a maze they'd turn to dust. Upon entering the maze, Daisy discovers something of value, something only she is able to retrieve that will help her on her mission to breaking the witch's curse.'

'Oh mum, you absolute genius!' I pick up the camera, make sure it's recording and enter the maze aware that auntie will be expecting me for breakfast anytime soon, and I had to make up an excuse for William's absence. Whilst walking I wonder what I'd find at the centre and feel tempted to cheat and read the rest of the story but a nagging voice in my head told me to only use it in extreme emergencies! Wow, wonder where that came from and felt a chill on my side. I smile, thinking it had to be Hans. I turn the corner, then another and keep going until I stumble into a dead end. I turn back, take the alternative route, and finally arrive in the centre of the maze, but I don't see anything but empty space and grass.

'You've got to be kidding me!' I huff. I'm so very tired now and really need sleep but there's no time for that even. I pace around the empty space tempted to look at the story but as I'm about to, the sun peeks over the mountains its golden light beams into the maze and lying on the floor seemingly out of nowhere is a large, rather tatty leather-bound book with silver gilded corners. I blink a few times incase I'm imagining it but it's solid, real and it's lying on the floor by my feet. I get on my haunches and reach out to touch it when I see what's written on there:

The Witchspell Family Book of Spells and Incantations

'Wow, what a book!' So, this must be the secret to getting us out of this mess. No wonder it has been hidden all this time. At that moment the phone goes off.

'Leave.'

'Huh?' I apologise into the camera as I was about to stuff it into my pocket and pick up the book, heeding the advice because so far, it's been pretty accurate. I make my way out of the maze and rush back to the manor shoving the book under my coat and as I walk through the door, auntie is walking down the stairs, yawning.

'Gosh! You're an earlier riser aren't you!'

'Yeah,' I say as casually as I could and head to the kitchen where auntie was going as well. 'Science stuff!' I laugh nervously and decide it's probably best to get up to the attic.

'Don't you want breakfast?' she asks. 'The party isn't until late this evening and I don't want you going hungry.'

'Um,' the book now feels weighty, and I really feel I might drop it if I don't get moving. 'I'll just get washed and I'll be down.'

'Oh Wend,' she turns back. 'How did the YouTube thing go last night. I was meant to watch it, but I... had other stuff to attend to.'

Hm, like what? I ask myself, but I bite my tongue. 'Oh, it went really well; I'm not convinced about ghosts yet though. Anyway, see you in a bit.' I dash upstairs as fast as the heaviness of the book would allow and rush up the steps to the attic. I put the book on my bed and take out the camera and sit down for a second and rewind the footage to where Bertha took William. I'm hoping to find clues, anything. The moment Bertha grew tall, William had dropped the camera, so the angle was facing the woods. I'm about to rewind, when I see movement in the trees and when I zoom in, I can see the witches standing around in a circle. I gasp. 'Did auntie really conjure Bertha?' Just then a rattling sound drew my attention to the bedside table. 'Elisa!'

Chapter Sixteen

As I reach to grab the bottle, which is said to contain Elisa's spirit, I feel a slight breeze and see the book has opened by itself and the pages are flipping erratically. After a moment it stops and is open on one particular page, so I assume it's important. Still holding the bottle, I lean over the bed and see the words in red ink: **The Underworld. A Beginner's Guide.**

'Underworld?' I look at the bottle as though Elisa is hearing every word and read on, inwardly dreading what I'm about to discover.

'The Underworld exists in a different dimension to our own. Humans cannot see it and cannot enter it without the aide of a spirit, but heed this caution. Once a human enters the underworld, they have less than a day to re-enter the human world or they will be trapped forever. A curse reversal spell will work for this. See page 119.'

'Oh my god, Bertha, what have you done?' Then, the page flips again and I read on. *'To undo a curse put on another by a witch you must take something personal belonging to the witch and perform this ritual on Halloween. The spell can only be undone before the clock strikes midnight.'*

'Something personal?' I say to the bottle and I'm beginning to feel slightly ridiculous talking to glass. I get to my feet, still holding the bottle and rifle through my brain what in the world could I find belonging to Bertha to break the curse AND bring William back. By MIDNIGHT!

'Have courage.' The voice on the app said.

'I need a cauldron full,' I laugh, but it was more nerves than anything. So, first things first, I need to show auntie that everything is fine, so she doesn't get any more suspicious than I already think she is, so I have to go down for breakfast and make an excuse for William's disappearance. I suck in a deep breath, throw on a clean jumper and brush the knots out of my long hair. I hide the bottle under the bed along with the book and walk downstairs as though I hadn't met a witch or a ghost in my life and that anyone who believes in such things are crazy. That ought to do it, I think to myself and remember that I had seen such things, things that I still find hard to understand. I catch a glimpse of myself in the dressing table mirror and look at my reflection. My tired green eyes stare back at me, and I barely recognise myself after everything I've seen the past day, then to the left I see a reflection of a man standing next to me wearing dungarees and a white shirt. His hair is short and blond, and he has the kindest face and smile.

'Hello, Hans,' I say. 'I promise you that I will free Elisa.'

He nods and then he's gone and for some reason I feel empowered as though years and years of the Witchspell women's strength and resilience surges through me making me believe that I can do anything I put my mind to.

I'm about to head out of the attic when mum sends me a message.

'I knew you could do this, Wendy. Elisa told me many years ago that she foresaw a girl coming into the family who will put things right. Those were her words and I know now she meant you.'

'But what about auntie? I saw her with Mari yesterday. Who is she?' It's at this point mum decides to video call me instead.

'Mari is our cousin. She's been helping Willie with the Halloween preparations as she does every year, because for the past twenty or so years, they've been trying to break the curse and find a way of recovering the Witchspell family spell book. But what we didn't figure out until recently is that it's only you who could find it, a girl of pure heart and intent, someone who would not use it for their own gain. Thanks to my Grandad, the book has been safe in his maze topped with my grandmother's spell.'

I suddenly feel so guilty for thinking auntie was a wicked witch in league with Bertha to the point I feel embarrassed to admit it to my mother, but good old mum has me figured out.

'Did you think Willie was the enemy?' she laughs. 'Oh Wendy, for a genius you are so silly.' She frowns. 'Wendy, where is William?'

I swear she's a witch! Oh, of course she is. 'Bertha took him. I saw it, Mum, it was awful and downright scary. The book says I need something personal of Bertha's to break the curse and the hexes and whatever else she's done...' I gasp, slightly out of puff.

'Something personal, eh?' she ponders on this for a moment whilst looking out of her hotel window. 'There's nothing in the house belonging to her that I know as she was booted out and it was made clear that all trace of her was gone.'

'Bones,' the app said.

'Bones?' Mum asks. 'Is that one of them ghost apps I hear?'

'Yeah, it's William's and what... Oh I know what it means, it means *her* bones! We found her grave in the woods, mum and what's left of her cottage!'

'Look for a spell in the book for a bone to appear on the earth if there isn't a bone already disturbed and out of the ground already.'

'Will do, Mum, thanks.'

'I'll speak to you very soon,' she says and then we say our goodbyes.

I didn't have to even rifle through pages because the book slid out from under the bed and opens on the very page. I snap a picture with my phone and head downstairs.

Chapter Seventeen

I go downstairs and as I get to the kitchen; I see the back of auntie sitting at the kitchen table but there's another person's shadow cast on the microwave. I hear a low murmur of conversation and as I step into the kitchen it stops and I see Mari sitting at the other end of the table holding a mug of something. Mari's eyes alert Auntie to my presence and she swings around in the chair.

'Wendy,' she sounds concerned. 'Come and sit down, I've just been talking to your mother.'

I glance at Mari and Auntie introduces us.

'Wendy this is Mari, but I believe you've already met, haven't you?'

'Yes, I'm sorry for trespassing on your property but we were only...'

She raises a hand and smiles. 'It's fine, Wendy. I knew who you were anyway, but I couldn't say anything as Willie will explain to you.'

'Sit down, Wend. I hear you had a rough night and poor old William...'

I settle down into the chair but I'm anxious to get moving, to get William back. 'Auntie I don't have time to sit and talk, I've got a spell to break!'

'I heard. Look, Wendy, please don't blame us but we couldn't say anything to you. It's something we hoped you would find out for yourself because well, you see everything so scientifically, that if we sat down and told you your family were witches you would've scoffed and maybe the book would never have been found.'

'I get it, but I really must be getting off...' I go to stand up and Auntie does too.

'Yes, I've managed to convince William's dad that he has spent the night ghost hunting and fallen asleep in the library. The poor man was poisoned by Bertha, can you believe it?'

'Actually, now I can believe it but if you asked me this yesterday, I probably would've scoffed!' I say.

'She even broke through my spell and has been hunting for Elisa's spirit, but she couldn't get the right bottle off the shelf because I put an invisibility charm on it.'

'Ah now I know why she wanted William and I to get it. If you're wondering where it is, it's safe in my room.'

Mari laughs. 'Genius!'

'Yes, she is. Well, Mari has given his dad medicine for it, so he's on the mend. Now, as for tonight... you know what you're doing?'

I shrug. 'I guess so, but first I need a bone of Bertha's. Actually, that's where I'm going now.'

Auntie nods. 'Yes, your mother told me that as well. If you need our help, we're here, okay?'

'I'll be fine. I'm a scientist,' I wink and leaves the house.

I'm back in the woods and this morning I'm extra vigilant. I open the photo album on my phone and read the spell again and again so I'm familiar with it and I don't have to hold the phone in case anything should happen. Weak sunshine filter through the leaves throwing dappled light on the now dried muddy path. There is a peaceful feel to the woods today, but I'm aware how light can also be deceiving.

Walking the trail to Bertha's grave I get several messages from mum and auntie to be extra careful and that I should've let someone come with me, but they understood it was my mission and that I was to get the bone and get back to the manor as quickly as possible.

As I approach the grave, I begin chanting the spell over and over. I don't know what I'm expecting to happen to be honest, perhaps a bone will shoot out of the earth or will appear there as if by magic, but I suppose it was better than digging the actual grave with a shovel because for some reason, even though she's wicked, it still felt disrespectful.

Standing next to the grave, I repeat the spell and as I'm halfway through I feel a slight rumble under my feet and a horde of crows fly out of the nearby tree, their flapping wings giving that extra chill to the scene before me. Then, as if I needed any more dramatics, the sunlight begins to weaken as a passing cloud casts a shadow over the grave itself and the dirt moves as though getting ready to dispel something. I step back and several moments later a bone materialises out of the ground and waits for me to collect it.

'Too easy,' I whisper. I suck in a breath and with a gloved hand I pull the bone out of the surrounding earth and place it gently into a bag. I send auntie a quick voice message.

'I've got it and I'm on my way back.'

'That was quick,' she replies almost instantly.

'Yeah, she literally jumped out of her grave,' I say and shiver at the thought of what I was carrying.

Chapter Eighteen

Arriving at the manor, I'm greeted with at least twenty brooms of varying shapes and sizes propped against the wall. I wonder if this is to do with the Halloween party but then I remember the flying witches from the previous night. I doubt very much auntie has ordered a horde of brooms to clean with and to be honest I don't have the strength to rationalise it, so I walk into the house and call for aunt.

She comes running out of the library. 'Have you got it?'

I hold up the bag. She steps back and regards it as if it were a smelly bag of dog poo. 'Here's Bertha, so now all we've got to do is perform the spell and bring William back and free the ghosts. Piece of cake, right?'

Auntie purses her lips. The silence spoke more than any word could've done. I inwardly groan at this because I am so done with it all.

'What now?' I ask.

'Well, you need to be part of the circle before you can perform a spell of that calibre, it's for your protection more than anything.'

'Oh, what does that involve?'

'Becoming an actual, proper witch,' she looks over her shoulder and it's then I notice the women standing around the library with eyes on me and realise who the brooms belong to.

'I thought being part of the family was enough. I did the spell for the bone, didn't I?'

'Yes, but that was lower grade level spell a gnat could do. You do realise you're bringing William back from the underworld? And if you're not highly protected you could get sucked in there?'

I roll my eyes. 'Fine, fine, can we get it over with please, I would like this over with before midnight so I can get some sleep.'

Auntie laughs. 'I would like that too. So, come out the back garden...'

'What does it involve?' I ask, getting worried. 'I don't have to eat frog legs and grow a crooked nose with a wart on it?' I laugh and realise one woman looks exactly like that. 'Oh, I meant no offence,' I say, stepping into the garden where a five-pointed star made of wood lay on the ground. Auntie informs me that the points stood for an element, such as earth, fire, air, water, and lastly, spirit, which encompasses it all.

'It's all natural, Wend, don't worry.'

'Oh, I'm not worried,' I reply, and truly, I wasn't.

The women gather around it forming a circle and auntie asks if I could step into the middle.

'It'll be over in a jiffy,' she winks.

As they gather around me a rumbling in the sky began and a strike of lightning flashes across a black cloud above my head.

'It's okay,' auntie calls out. 'We're calling in the elements to assist.'

I wasn't really worried as I knew a lot about weird weather patterns, too. This was perhaps a coincidence. And it's then began chanting...

We cast this circle

With pure intent

To bring in Wendy, our new friend

To do only good

And no harm

Please protect us oh charm

We bind this spell

For all now

Is well

As they stopped the cloud dissipated and the sun came out again blinding me with its light.

'Was that it?' I ask, feeling a little deflated. I expected to feel some kind of change within me, or maybe a boom and a puff of smoke to indicate that I am now a fully fledge witch, but nope. Magic can be a little disappointing it seems.

'That's it,' says auntie. 'Now, you must get that book and the bottle. Go!'

I sprint indoors and up the three winding staircases and then climb the attic steps, totally unprepared for what waited for me. 'How did you get in here?' I ask, looking at Bertha's human form, about to reach for the bottle.

She turns to me cackling so much you'd swear she's mad. 'You made one silly mistake, child. You brought my bone in here, rendering all the charms weak,' she cackles.

'Step away, Bertha. I'm warning you.'

'Oh, you're warning ME?' she laughs. 'What can a stupid child do to stop me? You couldn't even stop me taking your pathetic friend. Believe me, I'll be glad to get rid of the annoying...'

Out of nowhere, Pluto zooms into the room and leaps onto Bertha, hissing and scratching her face. I take this opportunity to grab the bottle and the book and get out of there.

'WILHELMINA!' I yell, and that's not like me as I never call her by her name but when I come downstairs, there's nobody here. It's as dead as a graveyard.

Then to my horror I hear...

DONG! DONG! DONG!

Outside it's already dark and when I turn to the grandfather clock it's struck 11.

'How?'

'A time charm, but you wouldn't know that would you being a... scientist!' she spat like it was a filthy word.

'I'm warning you Bertha. If you don't bring William back, I'm performing this spell, right here, right now because I'm not afraid of the wicked old witch.'

She walks around me in a circle and I'm getting oh so tired of this nonsense. Science is much easier except for the equations.

'Bertha, you're family. Why would you want to do this?' I try to reason with her.

'It's a matter of principle, girl. She wished me ill luck and I drowned, besides after helping her with her precious Hans, I think I'm due compensation.'

'No.'

'No what?'

'No to all of it. We do things for family and expect nothing in return because THAT'S what families are for. You put a curse on Elisa because you're just a nasty old woman.' I glance at the clock and it's now 11:15. When is she ever going to give up?

'Family? Family?' she shrieks. 'Even my own ousted me out of his will. This,' she gestures around the hallway, 'should be mine.'

'Well, it's not,' I open the book and the pages flip by themselves to the page I need. Sometimes magic can be amazing! Just then Pluto strolls in and walks up to Bertha. Now I know witches are supposed to like cats and all that because it's a thing, but Bertha literally jumps halfway across the room at the sight of her.

'Get that stinking cat away from me!' she yells, flinging her arms all over the place like she's about to be attacked by a grizzly bear not an ordinary domestic cat. Not that Pluto would attack her for no reason, of course.

'Why?' I yell back at her, and it's then I notice something strange happening to Pluto.

She grasps her throat at this point as if Pluto were making it hard for her to breathe. Is she allergic to cats I wonder, and then she screeches, 'Because... Because...'

Well, she didn't have to finish her sentence because Pluto, my beloved pet cat I've had since I was six, grows bigger and bigger until she forms the shape of a woman in Victorian dress. My mouth drops to the floor. Where has my beloved Pluto gone and who is this strange woman with piercing green eyes staring back at me? She has dark hair pulled up into a bun and she turns to smile at me as if she's known me my whole life and quite honestly; I feel like I know her, too. Weird.

'Do the spell, Wendy,' she says. 'Do it now...'

'But, but... Who are you?'

'Your great-great-grandmother. Now please, read it aloud.'

It was then I feel Hans' spirit drawing nearer, sending chills down my arm. I had a strange feeling come over me that he's here to support me.

I cast this circle
Of love and light
To bring forth
All my ancestors tonight
I break the curse
And set the spirits free
On this
All Hallows Eve

A blinding flash of light fills the room and the bottle cracks in my hand, leaving me holding the neck. It's then I see a white orb float from the bottle across the room and form into a woman, my great aunty Elisa. Then, to my right, a dark hole appears in the centre of the hallway like a blackhole in space and spits out William and sucks in Bertha. Thank goodness he's in one piece. And good riddance to Bertha.

'It's done, Wendy,' says my great great grandmother. But as all spells go, this is the sacrifice. I was sent here to protect you and now my job is done. It's been splendid to have been a part of your life and thank you for taking very good care of me.'

'Plu... I mean...' I'm so lost for words at this point, tears stream down my face. 'But I love you.'

'Love never dies, Wendy. This was meant to be.' She comes to hug me, and it feels like a real person.

Then, as the clock strikes midnight the hole disappears and I'm standing in the hallway in shock.

'What happened?' William says, rubbing his head. 'One minute I'm here and the next... I'm not even sure where I went.'

'Oh thank goodness you're okay. I'm so sorry you had to go through that.'

'No worries, I can't even remember where I went anyway,' he chuckles.

I sigh with relief at this and hope I never have to tell him one day. 'I've lost Pluto,' I say. 'Pluto's gone.'

'Oh Wendy, I'm so sorry,' he pulls me in for a hug.

'But I'm happy to see you again,' I say. 'And so will your dad. I really didn't want to have to explain this!'

'Thank you, Wendy,' says a woman's voice next to me and as I turn, I see her pretty green eyes and dark hair in victory rolls. She's wearing her ARP uniform, and her hand is tucked in Hans. For a ghost, she looks as good as her photograph, if not better.

'Elisa, it's so nice to finally meet you.'

'You are a true Witchspell, Wendy. I'm so proud of you for what you've done for us. If I can ever repay you one day, be sure to call on me.'

'Thank you, I will remember that.'

As she and Hans slowly fade away, I hear the song, 'We'll Meet Again,' as if being played by a band in the hall and when I look around, I see it busy with people in military uniforms like it was back in the 1940s. I'm well aware they're all spirits and it doesn't seem to faze me. Maybe the paranormal is becoming a normal part of my life... I laugh aloud at this and wonder if we'll be in for anymore surprises. Witchspell Manor is not the boring place I took it for, that's for sure.

William nudges me and smiles. 'You did it, Wendy. You broke the curse and now I'm going to tell everyone on YouTube you're my new best friend.'

I smile at this because this is exactly what I had wished on a star for. A friend.

Thank you for purchasing Wendy Witchspell and the
Impossible Ghosts. If you enjoyed this book, you may also like:
Wendy Witchspell and the Belligerent Bigfoot
Wendy Witchspell and the Furious Fairies
Wendy Witchspell and the Vain Vampires
Wendy Witchspell and the Whining Werewolves
Wendy Witchspell and the Avenging Angels
Wendy Witchspell and the Dastardly Demon

Milton Keynes UK
Ingram Content Group UK Ltd.
UKHW011804031123
431729UK00001B/25

9 798223 785026